Words to Know Before You Read

bridge

charged

except

fantastic

ignore

meadow

tasty

throughout

troll

yearly

www.rourkepublishing.com

Edited by Luana K. Mitten
Illustrated by Robin Koontz
Art Direction and Page Layout by Renee Brady

Library of Congress Cataloging-in-Publication Data

Koontz, Robin
 The Three Billy Goats and Gruf / Robin Koontz.
     p. cm. -- (Little Birdie Books)
 ISBN 978-1-61741-826-6 (hard cover) (alk. paper)
 ISBN 978-1-61236-030-0 (soft cover)
 Library of Congress Control Number: 2011924609

Rourke Publishing
Printed in China, Voion Industry
  Guangdong Province
042011
042011LP

www.rourkepublishing.com - rourke@rourkepublishing.com
Post Office Box 643328 Vero Beach, Florida 32964

The Three
BiLLy GOaTS and GRUFF

Written and Illustrated by
Robin Koontz

4

Three billy goats lived in a meadow. Everyone was friendly, except for a troll who lived next to the bridge.

The troll usually stayed inside his house. But on the first day of summer, he always came outside. He would pace back and forth over the bridge, yelling the same thing over and over.

7

So, on the first day of summer, everyone just stayed away from the bridge.

9

One spring day, the three goats found yummy flowers in a field across the bridge. They were so full after eating flowers all day that they decided to spend the night.

The next morning as the littlest goat tromped across the bridge the troll yelled, "Where do you think you're going?"

"I'm going home," said the little goat.

"First I'm going to have you for dinner!" said the troll.

"My brothers are coming!" cried the little goat.

"Good!" said the troll. "I will have them for dinner, too!"

13

"They will butt you with their horns," said the little goat.

"Well, that's the thanks I get," grumbled the troll.

"Why are you so grumpy?" asked the little goat. "You said you were going to eat us!"

"I did not!" cried the troll.

"Every summer the same thing happens," said the troll. "I tell everyone to come for dinner, and they ignore me!

Just then the other billy goats saw their little brother with the troll.
They put their heads down and charged at the troll.

17

"Stop!" yelled the little goat. "Mr. Troll just wants to have us OVER for dinner!" said the little goat.

"My name is Gruff," said the troll. "Would you please join me for dinner?"

The three billy goats and Gruff had a tasty meal.

Soon everyone found out that Gruff was a fantastic cook.

20

His yearly dinner party became famous throughout the land.

After Reading Activities

You and the Story...

What did the billy goats think that the troll wanted to do with them?

Why was the troll so grumpy?

Have you ever misunderstood what someone meant when they asked you something?

What could you do to make sure you do not misunderstand what someone is saying?

Words You Know Now...

Write three words from the list below on a piece of paper. Write a word that rhymes with each of the words. Now write a sentence including the original word and the rhyming word.

bridge	meadow
charged	tasty
except	throughout
fantastic	troll
ignore	yearly

You Could... Invite Someone New to Play with You

- Choose someone from school that you don't know very well.

- Invite this person to play with you at recess.

- Plan what you will do. Make a list of activities you can do together.

- Learn about your new friend by asking him questions about what he likes to do.

- Introduce your new friend to your other friends. Be sure to tell them something you learned about your new friend.

About the Author and Illustrator

Robin Koontz loves to write and illustrate stories that make kids laugh. Robin lives with her husband and various critters in the Coast Range mountains of western Oregon. She shares her office space with Jeep the dog, who gives her most of her ideas.